IZZY CAN'T TALK

Jennifer McGee
David Diamond

Published by Inclusive Art House, LLC
388 Bullsboro Dr. Suite 312
Newnan, GA 30263

Izzy is a little boy like other little boys. He lives on a small farm with his Aunt Bee and Uncle Gus, where he loves to play and have exciting adventures.

Izzy does lots of fun things,
but Izzy can't talk.

Izzy has autism, and can't communicate what he is thinking or feeling with his words.

Aunt Bee and Uncle Gus want to make him happy, but they can't always tell what he wants.

One day, Aunt Bee was making a delicious razzleberry pie. Izzy loves the taste of razzleberries.

Izzy wanted to say how excited he was for the pie, but he couldn't tell anyone because Izzy can't talk.

Izzy and Uncle Gus were playing a picture matching game while the pie was baking.

The smell of the pie was filling the kitchen. Izzy was getting so excited that he started rocking back and forth.

Uncle Gus was also getting excited for the pie.
He was breathing it in and licking his lips.

Uncle Gus just couldn't wait;
he had to taste that pie!
It was fresh from the oven
and the hot pie burned
his finger! "Ow! Ow! Ow!"

Uncle Gus yelled and hopped around the kitchen! Izzy laughed because he was doing a silly dance.

Aunt Bee heard the noise and rushed to the kitchen. "What's going on here?" she asked.

Aunt Bee noticed Izzy rocking. "Izzy, would you like some water?" she asked as she made the sign language gesture for water.

Izzy ran into the living room and started flipping the light switch.

He didn't want water; he wanted some pie.

Hey, buddy, why are you flipping the light?"
asked Uncle Gus.

"Maybe he wants to play pillow fort?"
Aunt Bee suggested.

"That's a great idea!
Come on Izzy! Let's stack the pillows!"
Uncle Gus said excitedly.

Aunt Bee showed Izzy a picture card.
"Do you want to play pillow fort?" she asked.

Izzy looked upset and started to jump. "Trampoline!" said Aunt Bee. "Maybe he wants to play on the trampoline." "It's worth a try," replied Uncle Gus.

Uncle Gus liked to jump almost as much as Izzy.
"Let's jump really high," exclaimed Uncle Gus.

Izzy didn't want to jump though.
What he really wanted was pie.

Uncle Gus ripped his pants while doing his trick.

Aunt Bee was thinking about what Izzy could possibly want. He didn't want water, to play pillow fort, or to jump on the trampoline.

Izzy's service dog, Lucky, brought something to Aunt Bee. "What do you have there boy?" she asked.

"It's Izzy's speech pad! Good boy Lucky, now Izzy can tell us what he wants!" Aunt Bee said.

Aunt Bee showed Izzy the speech pad and he pressed the 'Eat' button. Aunt Bee smiled because she finally knew what he wanted.

Izzy finally got his razzleberry pie, and it tasted delicious. He was so excited that he pressed the "Happy" button on his speech pad. Izzy can't talk, but he can communicate.

Dedicated to Our Sweet Isahiah,
who inspires us everyday.

A special thanks
to Matthew Diamond.

ABOUT THE WRITER AND ILLUSTRATOR

Jennifer and David are a real life mother and son team dedicated to sharing their talents working together in hopes of bringing awareness and greater understanding to the challenges of Developmental Delay and Autism. They look forward to creating more content together.

Jennifer is a full time creative visual Artist, entrepreneur, and parent to a special needs person. After her nephew Isahiah came to live with her full time she began to learn about his diagnosis's of Autism and Developmental Delay. Her understanding about the requirements of the special needs community led to her passion for advocacy and teaching. As she traveled across the country, she began observing the different strategies and practices the community and public policies have towards special needs and disabled persons. She also began educating herself by taking classes and joining many advocate groups to be better prepared to serve the disabled community through her talents of art and leadership.

David is an accomplished illustrator, animator and cartoonist. As a child he dreamed of making art for others to enjoy, in a variety of mediums such as drawing, painting, and sculpting. After completing an animation degree from Savannah College of Art and Design, his dream was fulfilled. He enjoys creating art and content that inspires others to enjoy life and be involved in the community.

Copyright © by Inclusive Art House

First Edition: December 2023

LCCN: 2023950992

ISBN Hardcover: 978-1-962636-00-1
ISBN Ebook: 978-1-962636-01-8

Published by Inclusive Art House, LLC
388 Bullsboro Dr. Suite 312
Newnan, GA 30263

Edited by: Theresa Burns, Carol Trow and Glenys Nellist
Designed by: Veronica Scott
Illustrated by: David Diamond

Visit our website for a free gift from Izzy
www.inclusivearthouse.com

Printed in the USA
CPSIA information can be obtained
at www.ICGtesting.com
LVHW061200070224
771186LV00019B/473